Jitterbug Jam

Barbara Jean Hicks

Pictures by Alexis Deacon

Farrar, Straus and Giroux
New York

Text copyright © 2004 by Barbara Jean Hicks
Pictures copyright © 2004 by Alexis Deacon
All rights reserved
First published in Great Britain by Hutchinson,
an imprint of Random House Children's Books, 2004
Printed and bound in Singapore
First American edition, 2005
3 5 7 9 10 8 6 4

www.fsgkidsbooks.com

Library of Congress Cataloging-in-Publication Data
Hicks, Barbara Jean.
    Jitterbug jam / Barbara Jean Hicks ; pictures by Alexis Deacon.— 1st American ed.
        p.   cm.
    Summary: Grandpa Boo-Dad not only believes that Bobo has seen a pink-skinned boy
with orange fur on his head hiding under the bed, he knows exactly how a little monster
can scare off such a horrible creature.
    ISBN-13: 978-0-374-33685-1
    ISBN-10: 0-374-33685-7
    [1. Monsters—Fiction.   2. Fear—Fiction.   3. Family life—Fiction.]   I. Deacon, Alexis, ill.
II. Title.

PZ7.H53153Ji 2005
[E]—dc22
                                                                            2004046981

To Lizzie Lou, Huckleberry, Mother Goose & Grimm
—B.J.H.

To Jacqui, for lending me her wardrobe
—A.D.

Nobody believes me,

and my brother, Buster, says I'm a fraidy-cat,
but I'm not fooling you:
there's a *boy*
who hides in my big old monster closet
all night long
and then sneaks under my bed in the morning
on purpose
to scare me.

I'm no fraidy-cat, neither.

Even Godzilla, who everyone knows
is the bravest monster ever,
would be scared of a boy
with pink skin
and orange fur on his head
where his horns by right should be,
and eyes that awful color the sky is
when you wake up in the middle of the day
and can't see, it's so bright out.

Yesterday was the scariest yet.

I hardly got a wink of sleep for all the *scritch-scratch-skittering* going on!

That's why I crawled in the cabinet under the sink this morning early,

still dark out

but coming on sunrise, when Mama always scoots us little monsters off to bed.

No bed for me.

Not with that scary boy . . .

just waiting.

Then Mama calls, "Hey, Buster, Bobo!"
I keep still as a stump in snow.

Not going to bed. Now nor never.

"You little monsters get on out here now," shouts Mama. "Boo-Dad's come!" Boo-Dad! Now what? Bed or no bed, boy or no boy, *got* to climb out for Boo-Dad.

So out I come.

No orange-headed boy about to show his face
with Boo-Dad round, nohow—
Boo-Dad the *biggest, baddest*
monster grampa ever.

Hey, Bobo!

And Boo-Dad grabs me up in a great big monster hug,
and quick as lickety-split 'n' spit-fish . . .

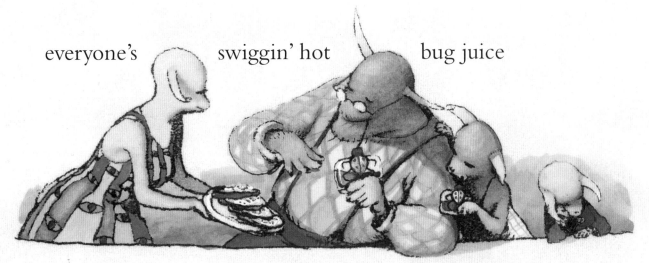

everyone's swiggin' hot bug juice

and scarfin' big old monster slabs of homemade bread with jitterbug jam
like they been starved since half past June!

Boo-Dad asks me how I been, and I tell him,

> Good mostly—
> not counting the scary boy
> underneath my bed.

Then what does Boo-Dad
do but scoop up me and
Buster and plop us down
on his big old monster
knees and start in on a
story about the olden days,
just like always.

"One time," he says, in a whispery way

that makes me all goosebumply,

 "one time when I was a little monster

and the sun was way up high in the

sky and Ma and Pa and Baby Boo

was all tucked in for a good day's sleep

and the house was tremblin'

with monster snores,

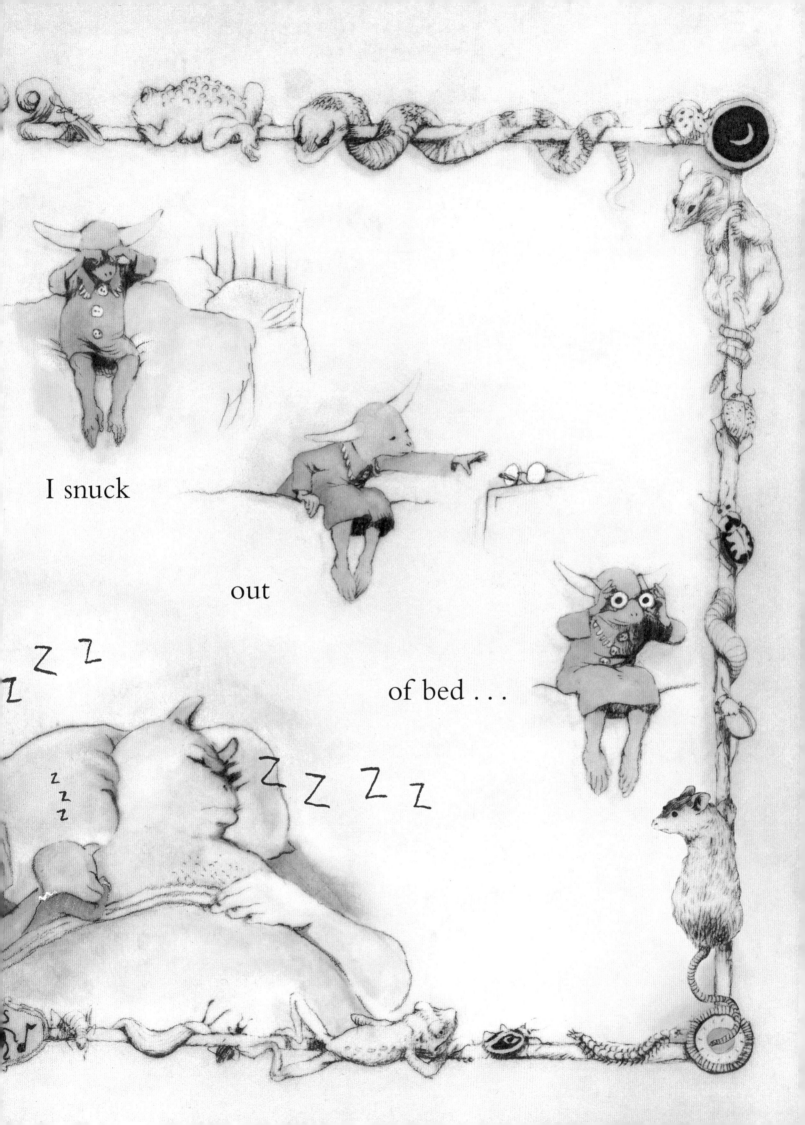

I snuck

out

ZZZ

of bed . . .

ZZZZ

. . . and across the floor . . .

and over . . . the windowsill . . . .

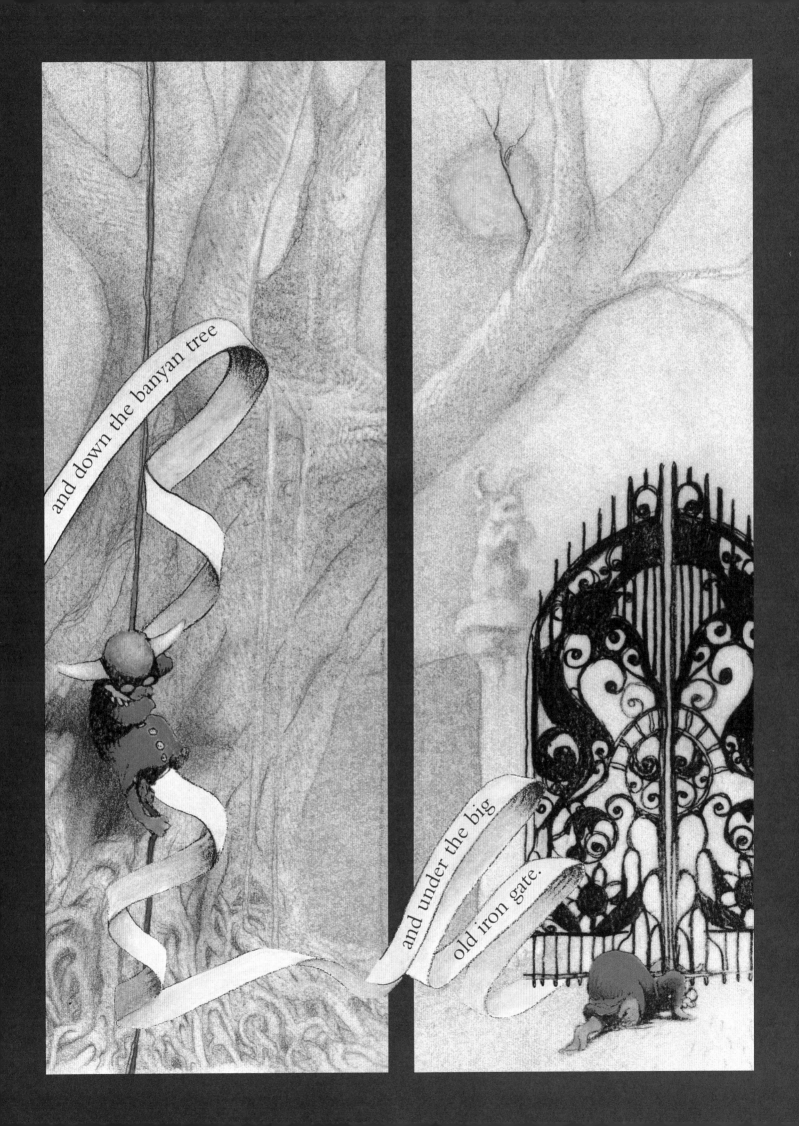

and down the banyan tree

and under the big

old iron gate.

And all of a sudden,
I'm in a garden of flowers
so dreaded cheerful
my blood runs hot
and my knees shake."

"A garden!" I says, all shivery.

"So what?" says Buster.
But then he says,
"What happened next?"

"You won't never believe,"
says Boo-Dad,
"what come trippin' along
the garden path."

"A boy!" I says.

"Close," he says. "A girl, it was—
which is almost just as scary,
but not quite."

"What did you *do*?" I says to Boo-Dad.

"Do?" says Boo-Dad.
"Run home fast as my monster legs
could carry me, that's what!"

"Scared, huh?" says Buster.

"Never more so," Boo-Dad says, straight to me,
 and he shakes his big old monster head.
"Wish I'd known then what I know now."

"What, Boo-Dad?"

"Best way to deal with a boy," he says,
"is to look him square in the eye.
 And then . . .

        you give him a great big toothy grin,

           and you say . . .

And you know what then?
Quick as lickety-split 'n' spit-fish,
that boy going to cringe, going to quake,
going to crumble like a week-old cookie!"

Not a minute goes by and I hear that

scritch-scratch-skittering

under my bed.

I start to curl up like a roly-poly,
but then I remember what Boo-Dad said.
I take a deep breath, lean over the edge.

And there he is . . .

the boy!
Pink skin,
orange fur,
and all.

I catch just a sparkle of sky-blue eyes
before I blurt out,

And I flash him a
great big toothy grin.

And you won't never believe what happens!
That boy yips
like I stomped down hard on his tail
(which is crazy as anything,
seein' as boys don't even have tails)
and he flings his arm up over his eyes,
and he says to me, mad as hornets,
"Hey! You trying to *blind* me?
You trying to turn me to fluff and dust?
Turn off that grin!"

I turn off my grin all right—but not because that boy says so.

It's *my* room. *I* make the rules.

Just about to tell him so, too,

when . . .

And I try to think how it would be
to play Hide 'n' Seek with Buster—
if Buster ever would stoop to play
with a monster as little as me.

"Shhhh!" he says. "Listen!"

Clump-Clomp-Clump-C

mp-Clump-Clomp-Clump-Cl

And quick as
lickety-split ’n’ spit-fish
he clump-clomps out of the closet
and round the bed
and into the closet again.
And he never seen a thing!

"Whew! That was close," says the boy.

"But where'd he come from?" I says.

"Other side of the closet," he says. "Same as me.
Thanks, kid! Under your bed
is the very best hiding place ever!"

And he jumps into my closet
and disappears.

I lie awake a long time after,
thinking about that boy . . .
how he has a brother
and plays Hide 'n' Seek
and says "please" and "thank you"
just like Mama taught me.

And I think about how that boy
must have a ma of his own,
and maybe a grampa like Boo-Dad
who tells him never, *ever* to
look at a monster's toothy grin,
or he's like to turn to
fluff and dust forever.

Then before I know it . . .

I wake up to a sliver of a moon
and the smell of bug juice brewing,

and I boogie out of bed and

hip-hop out of my jim-jams

and follow my nose to breakfast.

Buster's already there, scarfin' down worm and eggs.

"Hey, Buster," I says,
"let's play Hide 'n' Seek, why don't we?"
And he says,
like I'm lower than gum on his shoe,

"I'm no fraidy-cat," I says,
and I tell him about the orange-headed boy.

"Uh-huh," he says. "Some story, Bobo.
Ma, can I go now?"

That boy underneath my bed
don't know how lucky he is!

"Mama," I says after Buster's gone, "you ever hear tell of monsters and boys makin' friends?"

"Friends!" she says, like I just said the sun was the moon.

"Been thinkin'," I says, "'bout me and that boy hid under my bed."

"Oh, Bobo," sighs Mama.
"You and that boy!"

Yep. Me and that boy, all right.
I made up my mind,
and nobody going to change it:

come sunrise, going to slide
a slice of bread and jitterbug jam
                down under my bed . . .

. . . and see what happens.